THE SORCERER'S MAZE
JUNGLE TREK

by

Blair Polly & DM Potter

YouSayWhichWay.com

ISBN-13: 978-1546321392

ISBN-10: 154632139X

THE SORCERER'S MAZE
JUNGLE TREK

How This Book Works

This is an interactive book with YOU as the main character. You have entered the sorcerer's maze and have to find your way out again by answering questions and solving riddles.

You say which way the story goes. Some paths will lead you into trouble, but they all lead to discovery and adventure.

Have fun and follow the links of your choice. For example, **P34** means to turn to page 34. Or at any time, you can go to the List of Choices on **P96** and choose a section from there.

Can you find your way through the maze? The only way to find out is to get reading!

Oh … and watch out for the anaconda!

Enter the Jungle Maze

One moment you were at home reading a book and now you're standing in the jungle, deep in the Amazon rainforest.

Beside you flows a slow-moving river, murky brown from all the silt it carries downstream. Monkeys screech in the tall trees across the water. The air is hot and buzzing with insects. As you watch, the tiny flying creatures gather together in an unnatural cloud formation and then separate to form words:

WELCOME, they spell in giant letters.

You blink once, then again. This is crazy.

NOPE, IT'S NOT CRAZY, spell the insects. THIS IS THE START OF THE SORCERER'S MAZE.

The insect cloud bursts apart and the tiny creatures buzz off. What's next?

Twenty yards away, two kids, about your age, stand beside a small boat with a little outboard motor attached to its stern, and a blue roof to protect its occupants from the hot tropical sun.

They both smile and wave.

The girl walks towards you. "Do you want a ride upriver?" she asks. "My brother and I know the Amazon well."

"Do you work for the sorcerer?" you ask. "He designed the maze, didn't he?"

The girl nods. "Yes. My brother and I are his apprentices.

The sorcerer wants you to have company while you're here."

As the two of you move down the bank to the river's edge, the girl points to the boy. "This is Rodrigo. I'm Maria."

You drop your daypack into the boat and hold out your hand. "Hi Rodrigo, interesting looking boat."

Rodrigo shakes your hand. "It does the job. But before we can go upriver," he says, pulling a piece of paper out of his pocket. "The sorcerer wants me to ask you a question. If you get it right, we can leave."

"And if not?" you ask.

"I've got more questions," the boy says, patting his pocket. "I'm sure you'll get one right eventually." Rodrigo unfolds the paper. "Okay, here's your first question. Which of the following statements is true?"

It is time to make a choice. Which do you choose?

The Amazon River has over 3000 species of fish. **P4**

Or

The Amazon River has less that 1000 species of fish. **P7**

You need to go back to the previous page and make a choice by clicking one of the links. That is how you'll work your way through the maze.

The Amazon River has over 3000 species of fish

Piranha

"Correct," Rodrigo says. "And did you know that there are catfish that grow to over 200 pounds?"

Maria smiles, "And that's not even the biggest fish here. Arapaima can grow twice that size."

"And you want me to get in that rickety boat?" you ask.

The boy laughs. "Don't worry, we'll look after you. Now help Maria push off, we've got a lot of river to cover if we're going to make it to camp by nightfall."

As Rodrigo fiddles with the engine, you help Maria push the boat into the water, watching out for piranha as you do so. There aren't any proper seats in the tiny craft, so you sit on your pack near the middle, thinking that's where it will be the safest. Maria moves to the front of the boat to act as lookout.

The outboard motor starts on the first pull and Rodrigo

points the boat away from shore. Soon you are moving upstream about twenty yards off the bank.

Birds are everywhere. The jungle is alive with tweets and squawking.

As the boat comes around a bend in the river, you see a black and white bird about the size of a chicken sitting on a branch. The bird has a big orangey-yellow bill that reminds you of a banana split lengthwise. It has black eyes and a white patch on its throat. "Hey that's a toucan, isn't it?"

"We're lucky to see one," Maria says. "They usually stay way up in the canopy."

"What do they eat?" you ask.

"Mainly fruit, but they'll eat insects and snakes or even other bird's eggs if they need to. It depends on the season."

"The rains aren't far away," the boy says, looking at the overcast sky. "During the rainy season this place changes and the river gets so wide you can barely see across it."

The girl looks back at you. In her hand is a piece of paper. "And that leads us to our next question."

The boy slows the boat down. "Sorry, but if you get it wrong, I'll have to put you ashore."

You shoot a look towards the boy. "What? Here in the middle of the jungle?"

He nods, pointing to a track leading into the dense foliage on the near bank. "Don't worry. There's a track that leads to our next stop. You'll be able to rejoin us there."

You shrug. "Okay. What's the question?"

Maria reads the question carefully. "Approximately how

many inches of rain fall in the Amazon Basin each year?"

You scratch your head. How much rain does fall each year? It must be quite a bit if the river gets really wide.

It is time to make a choice.

Do 100 inches of rain fall each year? **P9**

Or:

Do 400 inches of rain fall each year? **P10**

The Amazon River has less than 1000 species of fish

"Unfortunately that's not right," Maria says. "The Amazon River has over 3000 known species of fish, and scientists are finding more each year."

"I never would have guessed that many," you say.

"I know. Not many people do. Don't worry, I have plenty more questions. I'm sure you'll get the next one right."

Another boat passes by, heading downstream. It's loaded with fruit for the market in a village downstream. The people in the boat wave as they pass.

Seeing all that food has made you hungry. You reach into the side pocket of your pack, pulling out a bar of chocolate. "Would you like some?"

Maria's teeth flash white against her caramel-colored skin. "Did you know that chocolate comes from the bean of the cacao tree which originated here in South America?"

"Really?" you say, unwrapping the bar.

Maria nods. "Now it's grown in tropical countries all over the world, but it started right here." Maria sweeps her arm indicating the jungle.

The boy and girl each take a piece of chocolate and bite into it. Their eyes sparkle.

The chocolate is soft and gooey from the tropical heat. It melts in your mouth.

"Seeing you've given us some chocolate," Maria says. "We'll give you another chance to answer that last question. Just don't tell the sorcerer."

"My lips are sealed." You smile and stuff the empty wrapper into your pocket.

Maria smiles and reads the question again. "So which is right?"

The Amazon River has less than 1000 species of fish. **P7**

Or

The Amazon River has over 3000 species of fish. **P4**

You have chosen 100 inches of rain

"That's a shame," Maria says. "We get over 400 inches of rain. Now we have to make you walk for a while."

"But…"

She looks a bit sad. "It's not up to us. The sorcerer makes the rules."

Rodrigo turns the boat towards shore. "Don't worry. If you follow the track, you'll get to where we're having lunch. Then you can ride with us again."

You step off the boat and scramble up the bank. By the time you turn around, the boat is already moving upstream.

The track is narrow and crowded with trees and shrubs. After walking for thirty yards or so, the jungle is so dense that you can no longer see the river, or hear the sound of the outboard.

When you come to a junction, you wonder which way to go.

It is time to make a decision. Do you go:

Left towards the sound of parrots screeching? **P12**

Or

Right towards where the jungle seems more open. **P23**

You have chosen 400 inches of rain

"Wow, you're good," Rodrigo says. "The Amazon's rainy season is from December to May. Boy, does it rain! Over 400 inches a year!"

You do some quick calculations in your head, dividing 400 by 12. "That's over 33 feet!" you say.

Maria nods in agreement. "Did you know that about twenty percent of all the fresh water that goes into the world's oceans comes from this one river?

"It's hard to imagine that amount of rain," you say. "Maybe we should set up an umbrella shop."

Maria smiles.

"The Amazon basin drains the land from over 7 million square miles," Rodrigo says. "No wonder it pumps out so much water."

"Look!" Rodrigo points to a snake lying in the shallow water near the bank. "I bet you can't guess the name of that animal."

The snake is a golden color with black stripes on its head.

"Wow that's big," you say.

Rodrigo grins. "About as big as they get," he says, swerving the boat for you to have a closer look. "If you get this next question right, you get to move on through the maze."

"And let me guess," you say. "If I get it wrong, you feed me to the snake?"

"Ha!" Maria laughs, "No, we'll just make you walk."

"So, what sort of snake is it?" Rodrigo asks.

It is time to make a decision. What do you think?

Is it:

A rattlesnake? **P14**

Or

An anaconda? **P21**

You have chosen left towards the sound of parrots

After turning left, you push through a few overhanging fronds towards the sound of parrots. As the squawking gets louder, you remember reading that some of the parrots living in the Amazonia rainforest are good mimics, which is why people like them as pets.

When you see a group of green birds sitting on a tree in a small clearing, you pull out your camera and take a few shots.

"Hello birdies," you call out to them, wondering if they'll reply.

One of the birds turns its head sideways and stares at your. Then it bounces up and down on its perch. "Hello birdie!" it squawks. "Hello birdie!"

You walk around the tree watching the birds, and then decide you'd better get going if you're ever going to catch up with the boat. Your stomach rumbles, reminding you that lunch isn't far away.

But which way do you go? There are four tracks leading out of the clearing.

You try to remember the turns you've taken and decide, as an aid to navigation, to pretend that the clearing is a clock face. You call the path you entered the clearing on the 6 o'clock path. There are other paths leading out of the clearing at 9 o'clock, 12 o'clock and 3 o'clock. But which do you take?

You are thinking hard, when you hear something large crashing through the jungle behind you. It could be a jaguar. There is no time to waste! Quick, which path do you choose?

Take the 9 o'clock path. **P26**

Take the 12 o'clock path. **P28**

Take the 3 o'clock path. **P30**

You have chosen Rattlesnake

"Oops," Rodrigo says. "There is a type of rattlesnake that lives in South America, but that beast over there is an anaconda."

"Let me guess," you say. "It's the biggest snake in the world."

Maria giggles. "How did you know?"

"Everything's big around here. Giant fish, giant otters, giant snakes. I suppose you'll show me the world's biggest spider next."

Maria raises her eyebrows. "That can be arranged."

"I was joking!" you say.

"Too late," Rodrigo says. "Look behind you."

Your eyes move first. Then you slowly turn your head and look around. "I hope you're kidding."

"The sorcerer aims to please," Rodrigo says looking down.

You follow his eyes and spot a hairy leg sticking out from under your pack in the bottom of the boat. Then you see another and another as the spider crawls out.

"Holy moly! What is it?" you say looking at the hairy black body. "It must be a foot long!"

Rodrigo nods. "It's a Goliath birdeater."

"Birdeater?" you say, moving further away from the hairy beast.

"It can also eat small rodents, lizards and frogs," Rodrigo says. "It has fangs an inch long."

As if the size of the spider wasn't enough to scare you, the thing starts hissing at you.

"Oh that's creepy! Can't you make it go away?" you say.

"Don't worry they're not deadly to people," Maria says pulling a piece of paper from her pocket. "Unless you're allergic." She raises her eyebrows. "Are you allergic?"

"How should I know?" you say, standing on your tip toes. "Just get rid of it!"

"Sure. All you have to do is answer this question."

"Okay," you say. "But read it quickly."

"Okay. Here it is. How does the Goliath birdeater make its hissing sound? Is it by:"

Releasing air out of its mouth? **P16**

Or

Rubbing its legs together? **P18**

16

You think the tarantula releases air from mouth to hiss

"Unfortunately that answer is incorrect," Maria says. "The tarantula makes a hissing sound by rubbing its legs together. But you're not the first to get that one wrong."

The spider runs towards you with a speed that rocks you back on your heels.

You are about to jump into the water when Rodrigo pushes it away with his oar.

"Phew!" you say. "That was scary."

"Imagine how you'd feel if you were a little mouse," Maria says.

After a moment, you stop shaking. "So what now? Are you going to put me ashore?"

Maria laughs. "Not this time. That was a pretty tough question."

You breathe a sigh of relief.

"But I am going to ask you another question. If you get this one wrong, you'll have to go back to the very beginning of the maze."

"Okay," you say. "Just promise to keep that spider away."

"I can't promise anything. It's the sorcerer that makes the rules," Maria says. "But I don't know why you're so worried. The poor spider's probably more afraid of you than you are of it."

You hand is still shaking. "I'm not so sure about that."

Rodrigo laughs nervously. "I'm not that fond of spiders either, so think carefully."

Maria pulls another question out of her pocket. "Okay here's an easy one. How many legs does a spider have? Is it:"

8 legs? **P18**

Or

6 legs? **P20**

Tarantulas hiss by rubbing two of its 8 legs together

"That's right. Tarantulas hiss by rubbing two of its 8 legs together," Maria says. "Did you know that you can always tell a spider from an insect by counting its legs. Spiders are arachnids with eight legs. Insects only have six."

"What are millipedes?" you ask. "Are they insects? They have heaps of legs."

Maria looks confused. "Hmm… I might have to ask the sorcerer about that one."

"I might do a search online about it when I get home," you say. "Insects sound interesting."

The tarantula crawls up the side of the boat. Rodrigo picks it up with the end of his oar and flicks it onto the shore. "They're all just bugs to me," he says. "They belong in the jungle, not on my boat."

You nod in agreement. "You're telling me."

Rodrigo, no longer distracted by the big spider, accelerates the boat and cruises along a row of trees overhanging the bank. "There are some good spots to see parrots around here," he says.

Now that sounds more like it. Parrots are your favorite birds. You've always wanted to own a parrot, so you could teach it to talk.

Half an hour later, Rodrigo nudges the boat into bank. "Here's where you get off if you want to see parrots."

You step ashore and scramble up.

"Just follow the track," he says. "It will lead you to where we're going to have lunch. We'll meet you there."

You wave goodbye and head into the jungle in search of birds, your camera at the ready.

The track is narrow and crowded with trees and shrubs. After walking for thirty yards or so, the jungle is so dense that you can no longer see the river, or hear the sound of the outboard.

When you come to a junction you wonder which way to go.

It is time to make a decision. Do you go:

Left towards the sound of parrots screeching? **P12**

Or

Right towards where the jungle seems more open. **P23**

Oops! You're back at the beginning at the maze!

How did that happen? You must have answered that last question wrong.

You are back at the clearing beside the river. Rodrigo smiles and waves as if he's never seen you before.

Maria walks towards you. "Want a ride up river?" she says. "My brother and I are trained guides."

"You work for the sorcerer." you say.

She looks confused. "How did you know?"

You shake your head in confusion as the two of you walk back down to the river's edge. You've been here before, but they don't seem to know you. You drop your daypack into the boat.

"Before we go upriver," Rodrigo says, pulling a piece of paper out of his pocket. "The sorcerer wants me to ask you a question. If you get it right, we can leave."

"And if not?" you ask, hoping you'll get the same question as last time.

"We'll just have to wait and see, won't we?" he says with a grin. "Okay, which of these statements is true?"

The Amazon River has over 3000 species of fish. **P4**

Or

The Amazon River has less than 1000 species of fish. **P7**

You have chosen Anaconda.

"Well done," Rodrigo says. "Anaconda is correct."

"Phew!" you say. "That's good, I didn't want to walk. There's so much more to see from the river."

"That's true," Rodrigo says. "But you still have a few more things to do before I can take you further upriver."

You're not too worried about more questions. You've been doing pretty well so far so you have no reason to think you won't continue to get the right answers.

"For your next challenge, I've got to put you ashore," says Rodrigo. "But don't worry; you can meet up with us again further upriver."

He nudges the boat into the riverbank and you scramble up.

"Where do I go?" you call to them.

"Just follow the path up the river," Maria says. "And try not to get lost. We'll see you at camp."

You don't like the sound of this much. "But what if I *do* get lost?"

The two of them laugh.

Maria shoves the boat away from the bank with an oar as Rodrigo starts the motor again. "Don't worry," she says. "The sorcerer will send a parrot to find you if it starts to get dark before you arrive."

The sorcerer will send a parrot? Why doesn't that comfort you? You lean forward and peer into the jungle. The path looks like a tunnel, with little light filtering down through the thick canopy.

When you turn back, the blue boat is disappearing around the corner, heading upriver.

"Oh well," you say to yourself. "I'd better get moving."

You follow the path until you come to a small clearing. In its center is a tree with a line of green birds sitting along one of its branch.

"Hello birdies," you call out to them, wondering if they'll reply.

"Hello birdie," one of them repeats, bouncing up and down on its perch.

After chatting with the birds for a few minutes, you decide you'd better get going if you're ever going to catch up with the boat. Your stomach is rumbling. You hope they've got some food onboard.

But which way do you go? The clearing is like a clock face with tracks at 12 o'clock, 3 o'clock, 9 o'clock and the one you came in on at 6 o'clock. Which trail will lead you along the river towards camp?

It is time to make a decision. Which one of these three paths do you take?

Take the 9 o'clock path. **P26**

Take the 12 o'clock path. **P28**

Take the 3 o'clock path. **P30**

You have chosen right towards more open jungle.

The path here is sunnier and more open. Parrots screech all around you as flashes of red, green, blue and yellow flit through the canopy.

After walking for about twenty minutes, you come to a big tree with a large branch hanging over the path. On it sits three birds.

At one end is a bird with teal-blue wings, a green patch on his head, and a yellow body.

"Macaw!" the bird squawks.

"Yes you are," you say. "A Blue and Gold Macaw."

The next bird along the branch is a brilliantly-blue bird with circles of yellow around its eyes and a flash of yellow on its face by its black curved beak.

"Macaw!" the bird screams.

"Yes you are!" you say to the beautiful bird. "You're a Hyacinth Macaw."

The birds bob up and down, looking at you. Then both birds turn to the third bird. This one has a red head and shoulders, and green, yellow and blue back and wings. You've seen pictures of this bird before, but have never seen so many colors on one bird in real life.

The bird looks down at you and squawks, "Macaw!"

"Yes you are," you say. "You're a beautiful Scarlet Macaw."

You whip out your camera. Nobody at home is going to believe you've taken a picture of three beautiful parrots all on the same branch!

"Macaw!" the first bird says.

"Macaw," the second bird says.

"Better get a move on!" the Scarlet Macaw says.

Did you hear right? Is that Macaw telling you to hurry up, or is the sorcerer playing mind games with you? In any case, the bird is right. You'd better get a move on if you're going to catch up with Maria and Rodrigo.

You head back into the jungle in a direction you think will lead you upstream. Ten minutes later, you come into another clearing where a group of green birds with yellow crowns sit on a bush. You point your camera and take a few shots.

These are Yellow-Crested Amazons.

"Hello birdies," you call out to them, wondering if they'll reply.

After photographing the birds for a few minutes, you decide you'd better get going.

But which way do you go? There are four tracks leading in and out of the clearing.

As an aid to navigation, you pretend that the clearing is a clock face.

You call the path you came in on the 6 o'clock path. There are other paths leading out of the clearing at 9 o'clock, 12 o'clock and 3 o'clock.

But which do you take?

As you wonder which way to go, you hear a large animal crashing through the jungle behind you.

Is it following your scent?

There is no time to waste!

Quick, which path do you choose?

Take the 9 o'clock path. **P26**

Take the 12 o'clock path. **P28**

Take the 3 o'clock path. **P30**

You have chosen the 9 o'clock path.

After a sip of water, you head out of the clearing, determined to catch up with the boat. You pick up your pace, sure that the path you've chosen will lead you back to the river. The path turns left, then winds around to the right.

Before long, the path narrows and you're not so certain you're going the right way after all.

After walking around another twenty yards, you pull aside a fern frond and hear a familiar voice.

"Hello birdie," a parrot says as you come into the clearing.

It's the same clearing you left only half an hour ago. How did that happen? You must have walked in a circle.

But which way do you go now? Which path is which? Is the 6 o'clock path still the 6 o'clock path or is it now the 12 o'clock path?

You head is spinning and you're wasting time turning around and around in circles.

"Better get a move on!" one of the parrots says.

You look up at a big fat green parrot sitting on a nearby branch. "What did you say?"

"Hello birdie," the bird says.

Maybe you're just hearing things.

"6 o'clock. Time for the news," another parrot says.

Is the sorcerer playing mind games with you? Or is the bird smarter than it looks?

None the less, the bird is right. You'd better get a move on.

But which way do you go? And which path do you take?

Do you:

Take the 12 o'clock path? **P28**

Take the 3 o'clock path? **P30**

Take the 6 o'clock path? **P32**

You have chosen the 12 o'clock path.

The sound of birds and bugs surround you. Small animal rustle through the undergrowth. You keep a sharp watch for potential danger as you move swiftly along the path. Suddenly, there is a crashing sound off to your right. Is something stalking you? And more to the point, is it dangerous?

Thinking of all the dangerous animals that live in the Amazonian rainforest just makes you more scared. Then you remember that mosquitoes, and the diseases they carry, harm more people than all the other animals put together each year. At least you can do something about that.

You stop, pull a tube out of your daypack and cover the bare patches of your skin with insect repellent before heading off again.

Every few moments you stop and listen for the sound of water, but the path winds around so much it's hard to know which direction you're going. Then after half an hour or so, you hear parrots.

A few minutes later your worst fears are confirmed: You are back at the clearing.

"Hello birdie," a parrot says in greeting. "Better get a move on."

But which way do you try next?

You look right, then left, then turn all the way around trying to figure out which path will lead you to the river.

You hold your hand up to your ear and listen, but all you

can here are the sounds of the jungle, the hum of insects and something snapping branches behind you.

It is time to make a decision. Which path do you take?

Take the 9 o'clock path. **P26**

Take the 3 o'clock path. **P30**

Take the 6 o'clock path. **P32**

You have chosen the 3 o'clock path.

Leaving the parrots behind, you head off into the jungle. It isn't long before the path narrows and starts to climb. If the path is climbing, you must be heading further away from the river. Not at all what you wanted.

The ground underfoot is damp and covered in leaf litter from all the trees.

You are starting to worry when at last the ground starts to head back down again. Maybe you've chosen the right path after all.

When you turn a last corner, you hear a voice.

"Hello birdie," it says.

Pulling a branch aside you find you've gone around in a big circle and are back at the clearing again.

"Hello birdie," another parrot says.

It's funny hearing the parrot talking, but you're concerned about the time you've wasted.

Which path should you take this time? You're well and truly stuck in the sorcerer's maze.

You went out on the 3 o'clock path, so you must have come back in on one of the others. But which is which? All you've managed to do is turn yourself around and lose all sense of direction. You are standing in the middle of the clearing, turning around and around wondering which way to go.

"Hello birdie," one of the parrots says. "Better get a move on."

The bird is right. You had better get a move on if you're going to catch up with Maria and Rodrigo.

Which of the paths do you take this time?

Take the 9 o'clock path. **P26**

Take the 12 o'clock path. **P28**

Take the 6 o'clock path. **P32**

You have chosen the 6 o'clock path.

This path looks like all the others. In fact, you're pretty sure you've been here before. But then you hear faint splashes ahead of you. Is it the river?

Excited to have found the river at last you start jogging. The splashing in the river gets louder and louder. But what's making the noise? Is it an animal or people?

You pull some low hanging branches aside and peer out over the river. There is something large and pink, in the water off to your left. You wait till it surfaces again. Then you see what it is. It's one of the rare pink river dolphins. So beautiful… You stand transfixed as the creature darts back and forth catching its lunch.

When you scramble along the path for a clearer view, you discover Maria and Rodrigo sitting on a log preparing food.

"So you made it," Maria says. "We always stop here to watch the dolphins."

"Not many of them left unfortunately," Rodrigo says. "Would you like something to eat?"

It feels like you've been walking for hours. You take the piece of yellow-green fruit the boy offers and bite right in. It's about the size of a tennis ball. The flesh is pink and sweet. Juice runs down your chin.

"Mmmm… that's good," you say. "What do you call it?"

"Ah now there's a question if ever I heard one," Rodrigo says, his eyes twinkling.

You hear the girl laugh as she pulls a piece of paper out of her pocket. "Yes, I seem to have a question on that topic right here."

"I should have known." You groan and take another bite. "But if you give me another one of these, I'll answer all the questions you like."

Rodrigo tosses you another piece of fruit.

"Okay," Maria says. "If you want a ride in the boat, all you have to do is name the fruit you're eating."

It is time to make a choice. Did you just eat a:

Plantain? **P34**

Or a:

Guava? **P36**

You have chosen plantain.

Well as you can see, plantains are like bananas and not the shape of a tennis ball at all. The correct answer was guava. Plantains are a very important fruit for those living in the Amazon basin. Often they are roasted on an open fire or cut lengthwise and fried.

"Looks like you're still walking," Maria says. "That's a shame. I was enjoying your company."

"Couldn't I have another question?" you ask.

The two of them whisper in each other's ear for a moment.

It's Rodrigo that speaks first. "Okay we can give you another question, but if you get it wrong you'll have to go all the way to the beginning of the maze.

"All the way?"

He nods. "Still interested?"

You think a moment. "Yes," you say. "Surely I can't get

two in a row wrong."

"Okay, here it is. What is the name of the largest predator in the Amazon basin?"

Is it the:

Black caiman? **P40**

Or

Tiger shark? **P46**

You have chosen guava.

"Looks like you get to ride in the boat again," Maria says. "Guava is correct."

"Birds like them too," her brother says. "And the monkeys."

You smile. "Well I'm not surprised, they're delicious."

After the three of you finish eating, Rodrigo and Maria return to the boat.

You rinse your hands in the river and climb aboard. "So, will we see many monkeys as we head up river?"

Maria nods. "You like monkeys?"

"And birds," you reply. "I saw some parrots in the jungle when I was walking."

Just as Rodrigo is about to say something, a brown furry face pokes out of the water about 20 yards away.

He points. "Hey look, it's an otter."

"Wow, that's huge!" you say.

Maria laughs. "They don't call them giant otters for nothing. They're the biggest in the whole world."

You're not surprised. This one looks about six feet long and weighs more than you do. "I thought they were endangered?"

"They are," Rodrigo says. "But the sorcerer asked this one to visit us so you could see how amazing they are."

The face dives under the water. Thirty seconds later, the otter back holding a fish between its paws. Floating on its back, it bites into its lunch.

"As you can see, they eat a lot of fish," Maria says. "A big one can eat 10 pounds in a single day!"

After the otter finishes the fish, it swims closer to the boat.

"They're inquisitive animals," Rodrigo says. "Unfortunately hunters nearly wiped them out for their fur."

"Destroying their habitat doesn't help either," the girl says. "People need to think more about the animals before they chop down the forest or build mines."

As you watch the otter, it is joined by four more. "Hey look. The rest of the family has arrived."

Rodrigo points to a hole in the river bank. "I think that's one of their dens over there. They live in big family groups."

Maria laughs as the otters frolic in the water.

"Anyway, it's time to go," Rodrigo says. "We've still got some distance to make before we get to camp."

When the motor starts, the otters swim off in search of more fish and Rodrigo points the bow of the boat back out into the river.

You sit down on your pack and watch the miles flow past.

"So you'd like to see some monkeys?"Maria says as she sits down beside you. "Any particular favorites?"

"Spider monkeys are cute," you reply. "I like chimpanzees too, but they're only in Africa."

"We also have lots of marmosets, dozens of different tamarins, howler monkeys and squirrel monkeys," she says. "Squirrel monkeys live in big groups."

"That's right," Rodrigo says. "I saw a group of about 500 squirrel monkeys once."

"That's the population of a small town," you say.

"Squirrel monkeys are small though," Maria says. "You could hold a full grown one in the palm of your hand."

You hold out your palm and try to imagine a monkey sitting there. "Wow that is small. I have so many questions. Maybe you could answer some of them?"

"Speaking of which," Rodrigo says. "If you want to get through this maze, it's time to answer another one."

You sigh. "Or you'll put me ashore?"

"Sorry," he says with a shrug.

"Okay, let's get it over with. What's the question?"

He pulls a piece of paper out of his pocket. "This one is more of a riddle, so listen carefully."

You nod.

"Right. If you start with 3 spider monkeys, add 4 tamarins and 3 squirrel monkeys, what is the total number of appendages the monkeys have?"

"Hmmm, appendages. Aren't they arms and legs?

"Maybe," he says. "It's certainly something that can grab hold of things."

"Okay," you say. "Let me think a moment."

It is time to make a decision.

Do 3 spider monkeys, 4 tamarins, and 3 squirrel monkeys have:

40 appendages in total? **P47**

Or

50 appendages? **P44**

You have chosen black caiman.

"Correct! Looks like you get to ride in the boat again," Maria says.

You pump the air with your fist. "Yes!"

Maria giggles. "Did you know that black caiman can grow up to sixteen feet long? Their black scaly skin acts as camouflage when they're hunting prey along the river."

"Sixteen feet long? Wow, that's big," you say.

"Females can lay up to 65 eggs at a time. Now's about the right time of year too, just before the rainy season. The eggs take about six weeks to hatch."

Once the three of you have finished eating your lunch, the Rodrigo and Maria return to the boat.

You rinse you hands in the river, then help Maria push the boat into the water and climb aboard. "Will we see many monkeys as we head up river?"

Maria nods. "Heaps!"

"Excellent. I love monkeys ... and birds," you say. "There were lots of parrots in the jungle."

Just as Rodrigo is about to say something, a brown furry face pokes out of the water about 20 yards away. "Hey look, it's an otter."

"Oh that's so cute! And big!" you say.

Maria laughs. "They don't call them giant otters for nothing! They're the largest otter in the whole world."

You're not surprised. This one looks bigger than you. "I thought they were endangered?"

"They are," Rodrigo says. "But the sorcerer wanted you to have a treat."

The otter dives under the water. Thirty seconds later, it's back holding a fish between its paws. Then it throws the fish into your boat and dives again.

"Looks like dinner is sorted," Rodrigo says.

"The otter resurfaces, floats on its back and bites into its lunch.

"As you can see, they eat a lot of fish," Maria says. "A big otter can eat 10 pounds in a single day."

After the otter finishes eating, it swims closer to the boat.

"They're inquisitive animals," the Rodrigo says. "Unfortunately hunters nearly wiped them out for their fur."

"Destroying their habitat doesn't help," his sister says. "People need to think more about the animals before they chop down the forest or start mining."

The otter flips over and dives again.

"Anyway, it's time to go," Rodrigo says, we've still got a

few miles to travel before we get to camp. He pulls the cord and starts the motor.

As the otter surfaces with another fish, Rodrigo points the bow of the boat back out into the river.

"So you'd like to see some monkeys?" Maria says. "Any particular favorites?"

"Spider monkeys are cute," you reply, "and golden tamarins."

"We also have lots of marmosets, dozens of different tamarins, howler monkeys and squirrel monkeys," she says. "Squirrel monkeys live in big groups."

"That's right," her brother says. "I saw one troupe of squirrel monkeys that must have had 500 in it."

"That's not a troupe," you say. "That's a crowd."

"Squirrel monkeys are small though," the girl says. "You could hold a full grown monkey in the palm of your hand."

"Really? I have so many questions I'd like to ask you about them," you say.

"Speaking of which," Rodrigo says. "If you want to get through this maze, it's time to answer another one."

"Or you'll put me ashore again, I suppose?"

"Sorry," he says. "But it's the sorcerer who makes the rules, not me."

"Okay, so what's the question?"

He pulls a piece of paper out of his pocket. "This one is more of a riddle, so listen carefully."

You nod.

Rodrigo reads. "If you start with 3 spider monkeys and

add 4 tamarins and 3 squirrel monkeys, what is the total number of appendages the monkeys have?"

Do they have:

40 appendages in total? **P47**

Or

50 appendages? **P44**

You have chosen that the monkeys have 50 appendages.

"Well done," Maria says. "Most of the people who've come into the maze forget that a monkey's tail is an appendage too. They're not just arms and legs you know."

As Rodrigo steers the boat further upstream Maria shows you a picture of a golden lion tamarin. "Some people think tamarins are a type of fruit and not a monkey."

"Sounds a bit like mandarins." you say, "so I'm not surprised"

"It does." Maria says. "And tamarind, the fruit has a 'd' at the end."

You stare at the monkeys. "They look about the size of a squirrel."

"I suppose they are," Maria says. "But there are quite a few different types. I like the emperor tamarin best, with its funny white mustache."

"Tamarins are pretty," Rodrigo says as he scans the river bank, looking for more animals. "But if you're looking for color, the birds win hands down."

The area around the river is a busy place. Birds chirp and squawk nearby and you hear splashes further upstream. You're pleased to be in the boat when Rodrigo points out a shoal of piranha attacking something in the water up ahead.

"Looks like a dead capybara," he says. "Piranha are a lot less vicious than the movies make out. They rarely attack larger animals unless they are already dead or dying."

"Really? What about people?" you ask. "I thought they

could strip you to the bone in minutes."

The girl smiles and shakes her head. "Hollywood has a lot to answer for. Piranhas swim in groups, mainly for their own protection. There's safety in numbers when you're a fish. But even so, they're often eaten by caimans, birds and otters."

"What's a caiman?" you ask.

The boy smiles and reaches into his pocket. "It just so happens I've got a question that relates to that."

You should have known. Every time you ask a question, these two sorcerer's apprentices come back with one of their own.

As you watch the piranha finish off the capybara, the boy gives you a serious look. "If you get this next question you can go to our jungle camp."

"What happens if I get it wrong?" you ask.

The boys points to shore. "Back into the jungle on foot I'm afraid."

You cross your fingers behind your back and hope the question isn't too hard. Some time in camp and a bit of a rest, sound just what you need.

"Okay, here we go. Caiman are the largest predator in the Amazon basin. But are caiman related to alligators or sharks?"

It is time to make a decision. What do you say?

Caiman are related to sharks. **P46**

Or

Caiman are related to alligators. **P48**

Oops. That's wrong. You are back in the jungle.

In a puff of smoke, you find yourself back in the clearing with the parrots.

"Hello birdie," a parrot says

"Hello birdie," you reply. "Now get lost."

"Get lost. Get lost. Get lost!" the parrot repeats, bouncing up and down on his branch.

"Quiet birdie, I'm trying to think."

"Quiet birdie!" the parrot squawks. "Quiet birdie. Quiet birdie. Better get moving!"

The bird is right. You'd better get moving.

But which way do you go? Which path is which? You're all turned around again.

Do you:

take the 12 o'clock path? **P28**

take the 3 o'clock path? **P30**

take the 6 o'clock path? **P32**

take the 9 o'clock path? **P26**

Oops. 40 appendages is wrong.

Rodrigo pull a picture of a spider monkey out of his pocker. "What about the tails?" he says pointing at the monkey's backside. "Tails are appendages too. Now I've got to send you back."

"Do you really?" You ask.

He nods. "At least you'll find a friend there."

"Will I?"

He smiles. "Yep."

In a puff of smoke, you are back in the jungle clearing with the parrots.

"Hello birdie!"

The boy was right. Your old friend the parrot is here.

"Hello, hello, hello," the parrot says as it bounces up and down on its branch. "You'd better get moving."

But which way do you go? Which path is which? You're all turned around and every path looks the same.

Do you:

take the 12 o'clock path? **P28**

take the 3 o'clock path? **P30**

take the 6 o'clock path? **P32**

take the 9 o'clock path? **P26**

Welcome to Camp 1

"Welcome to Camp 1," Rodrigo and Maria say in unison.

You smile as you look around. The place is pretty basic. Green tarpaulins are strung up between the trees with nylon cord to provide shade.

A wooden crate filled with cans of food and cooking utensils sits on the ground next to a campfire. A picnic table with bench seats sits nearby and acts as camp kitchen and dining room. Pitched off to one side of the covered area is a large tent with mosquito netting on its windows.

Maria smiles and walks towards an ice chest sitting under the table. "Like a cold soda?"

With a rattle of ice cubes she pulls out a bottle. Beads of moisture run down the bottle's side.

"How did you get ice way out here in the middle of the Amazonia rainforest?" you ask.

Rodrigo laughs. "It's the sorcerer, silly. He just snaps his fingers and things appear."

"Saves going to the supermarket I suppose." You take a soda and raising it to your lips. "Ahhhh, that is so good."

Maria and Rodrigo grab a soda each and the three of you sit down at the picnic table.

"So what now?" you ask.

You glance down as Rodrigo pulls yet another piece of paper out of his pocket. "Have you got an endless supply of questions in there?"

"I'm not sure," he says. "They just appear whenever I need one. The sorcerer's pretty good at this maze stuff."

You have to admit that the questions you've had so far have been interesting. "So what is it this time? More about animals?"

Rodrigo shakes his head. "No this one is about... Well you'll see. I'd hate to ruin the surprise. If you get it right you get to sleep in the tent."

"And if I get it wrong?"

He shrugs. "I'm not quite sure. We'll just have to wait and find out."

"Are you sure you don't know?" you ask, searching Rodrigo's face.

"I promise," he says. "I'm just an apprentice. The sorcerer only tells me what I need to know. Sometimes I'm as surprised as you are with what happens."

Spreading out the piece of paper on the table in front of him, Rodrigo starts reading. "Okay here we go. Brazil is the world's largest producer of what common product? Is it:"

Coffee? **P50**

Or is it

Tea? **P68**

You have chosen coffee.

"Well done!" Rodrigo says. "On the other side of the question paper is a picture of a coffee plant. Brazil has over 10,000 square miles of coffee plantations. That's quite a lot don't you think?"

"Yeah I suppose it is," you say. "Doesn't China produce the most tea?"

Rodrigo nods. "Yep." He walks over to the tent and lifts the flap. "Now you can make yourself comfortable, away from the mosquitoes. We'll be leaving camp early so I hope you sleep well."

"What about you and Maria?" you ask Rodrigo. "Where will you stay?"

"When the sorcerer snaps his fingers, we'll be transported home for the night," he says.

"You mean I'll be here alone?"

"I'm afraid so," Rodrigo says. "But don't worry. At least you won't be sleeping in the open. I've even left you some sandwiches in case you get hungry."

Things could be worse. You step inside the tent and look around. There is a camp bed with a thin mattress and a flashlight. Nothing else.

"What about blankets or a sleeping bag?" you ask.

"Way too warm for that," Rodrigo says with a chuckle. "We're almost at the equator. It's nearly as hot at night as it is during the day."

You try out the bed. "Not bad — for the middle of

nowhere."

After eating a sandwich, you lay on the bed and close your eyes, planning on having a five minute nap before going back outside to where Rodrigo and Maria are sitting at the table cooking pieces of fish on long sticks over the fire. But when you open your eyes again, it is dark and you can hear rustling in the jungle all around you.

"Rodrigo?" you call out. "Maria?"

There is no reply.

You figure the sorcerer must have snapped his fingers and whisked them home.

Quietly, you sit and listen to the sounds of the jungle.

The frogs are the loudest. If you listen carefully, you can hear at least ten different calls.

Some sound almost like crickets chirping, while others are deep booming rumbles.

On the ground, sitting on your empty soda bottle is a little green frog. It stares up at you with big black eyes.

"Ribbet!" the frog says.

After a few more croaks, the frog springs towards you. But rather than landing on you, there is a puff of smoke and the frog turns into a piece of paper which flutters down onto your lap.

You look at the paper expecting another question from the sorcerer, but there are only letters on the page.

And not just one or two letters, but a whole block of them!

It doesn't seem to make any sense.

Or does it?

> ueieuyjmdniklokslksj
> oieioejlookaroundjkd
> slookoopoeedds;woej
> dkdfjedklookarounds
> slslookaroundklitvxjf
> aledkdxmksieurtedlljk

After staring at the paper for a few minutes, you hear something rustling around the camp. You're unsure of what to do. It is time to make a decision. Should you:

Look around? **P53**

Or

Go back to sleep? **P66**

You have chosen to look around.

You've seen the secret message in the block of letters so you grab the flashlight and start looking around. It is pitch black apart from the dull glow of the fire. You throw on a few more logs and sit at the table.

Suddenly the frogs go quiet. Has something disturbed them? You sit a still as a rock and listen. There is rustling in the jungle not more than ten yards away.

Your eyes strain as you peer into the darkness. The shadows make all sorts of shapes. Did something just move? Lying beside the fire is a branch used for poking the embers. You stretch down and grab it.

Holding its blackened point towards the source of the noise, you hold your breath, expecting a wild beast to come charging forward at any moment. Then, after another rustle, you see a pair of golden eyes peering back at you.

Is it a jaguar? Are you about to become animal food?

Holding the stick like a spear, you huddle closer to the fire, never taking your eyes off the pair of eyes staring back at you.

"Meow!"

What? That doesn't sound like a jaguar.

Then you see it. It's a black housecat. How did a cat get out here in the jungle? You crouch down and hold out your hand. "Here puss, puss, puss."

The cat runs over and rubs its face against your hand. Then it starts purring.

"What are you doing out here kitty?" you ask.

The cat sits and looks up at you. It's as if it understands what you are saying.

"Are you the sorcerer's cat?" you ask.

"Meow," says the cat, rubbing against you once more.

"Did the sorcerer send you here to give me a message?"

The cat springs forward and, in a puff of gray smoke turns into a paper airplane which flies around in a big loop and then plonks into your lap. You unfold the paper. You suspect it's going to be another question about Brazil. But you're wrong. There are numbers on the page. It's a math problem with four numbers and a blank space. The note says:

WHAT IS THE NEXT NUMBER IN THIS SEQUENCE?
ANSWER CORRECTLY AND YOU'RE IN FOR A BIG SURPRISE.
GET IT WRONG AND YOU HAVE TO GO BACK
TO THE BEGINNING OF THIS LEVEL.

2 …4 …8 … 16 …__?

Is it:

22 **P85**

24 **P93**

32 **P74**

36 **P85**

What animal is this?

Maria giggles. "Oops. Looks like you're back at the start. I thought you said you knew animals?"

"I do normally," you say scratching your head.

"At least you get another go. So, do you remember what animal this is?"

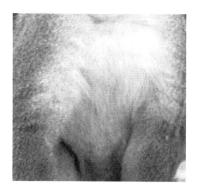

A Baboon? **P101**

Or

A Spider Monkey? **P56**

56

Spider monkey is correct.

"Well done," Maria says. "You got that right. Did you know that all seven species of spider monkeys are under threat and that the black-headed and brown spider monkeys are on the endangered list? It's so sad."

"I read somewhere that spider monkeys are the most intelligent new-world monkeys," you say. "I can't understand why people aren't more careful."

Maria nods. "Spider monkeys make lots of different sounds too. Did you know that they bark like a dog when they are threatened? Now get this one right or back you go."

You are imagining a spider monkey chasing your mailman down the street when Maria pulls another picture out of her pocket.

"Okay, so what do you think this is a picture of?"

Is it a:
Giant Otter? **P55**
Or
Piranha? **P57**

Piranha is correct.

Rodrigo hands you a guava. "Well done. Have a snack."

"Yes. Well done, smarty pants," Maria says grabbing a guava for herself.

As you bite into the fruit, you suspect Maria is about to tell you more about the well known fish.

"Scientists think there might be as many as 60 different species of piranha," she says. "The locals use their sharp teeth to make weapons."

Rodrigo turns to you. "Did you know that in 2013, on Christmas day, 70 swimmers in Argentina were attacked by piranhas? But attacks are rare," he continues. "So don't worry, normally they just take little fishy nips at you."

Then Maria turns over another photo. "Okay, clever clogs. What's this?"

Anaconda? **P58**
Or
Turtle? **P55**

58

Anaconda is correct.

"Wow!" Maria says. "You're on a roll. I can see I'll have to give you a trickier question next time.

"What? No lecture on anacondas?" you say

"I can if you want me to…"

You hold up a hand. "No that's alright," you say. "I already know it's the biggest snake in the world."

"But did you know that anaconda refers to a group of snakes and that it's the green anaconda that's the biggest?"

Then she flips over another picture. "Okay so what is this?"

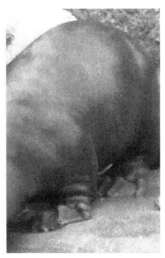

Hippopotamus? **P55**

Or

Giant Otter? **P59**

Giant otter is correct.

"Good guess," Maria says. "You must have seen the webbed feet. Hippos have four toes that aren't webbed, unlike the otter."

You smile. "Yeah and those legs looked a bit short for a hippo. Besides, hippos live in Africa, not South America."

"Very clever. But now it's time to test you on birds," Maria says turning over the next picture. "Over 1500 bird species are found here in the Amazon rainforest. Here's a picture of one you should know."

"You'd better get this one right," Rodrigo says with a wink. "If not, you be going back."

Is it a:

Myna bird? **P85**

Or

Toucan? **P60**

Toucan is correct.

"Aren't toucans amazing?" Maria says. "Did you know their beaks come in a variety of colors? Some have yellow or blue or green or black or even a combination of colors."

Rodrigo points at a toucan flying past. "Did you see that?"

You nod. "It's a wonder they can fly with that big beak."

"Their beaks might be long," Maria says. "But they're a lot lighter than people think. They have heaps of tiny air pockets in them to keep the weight down."

You're impressed with Maria's knowledge of birds and wonder which one she'll show you a picture of next.

"Okay, here's one you might remember," she says turning over another picture. "What is this?"

Scarlet Macaw? **P61**
Or
Red Lorikeet? **P93**

Scarlet Macaw is correct.

"Like toucans," Maria says. "Macaws come in all sorts of colors. They're very clever birds too."

As if to illustrate her point, a scarlet macaw comes and sits on a nearby branch. "Hello!" it squawks.

"Hello birdie," you reply.

"Birdie wants a sandwich!"

You look at Maria, then down at the uneaten crust of bread lying on the table. "Is it okay to feed the bird?"

She smiles. "Normally it's not a good idea to feed wild animals, but this is one of the sorcerer's pets so I suppose it's okay."

You toss the crust into the air. The bird flies up, catches it in its beak, and then soars up into the canopy.

"Time for your next picture," Maria says. "I might try something different this time. See if I can fool you and send you back to the start."

"Aw!" you say. "Don't you want me to finish the maze?"

"I do, but I'd like to keep you around for a little while longer. Otherwise the only friend I have is my brother and he's not much fun."

"Hey!" Rodrigo says. "I am too fun!"

"Okay, well you pick a photo then," she says to her brother.

"Right, I will." Rodrigo sorts through the pile, and then turns over a picture. "Okay what is this?"

You study the image. "How am I supposed to tell how

big it is from that? Can you give me a hint about how long the animal is?"

"Sure," Rodrigo says. "This one's approximately 14 feet long and it's a reptile."

Is it a:
Anaconda? **P55**
Or a
Caiman? **P63**

Caiman is correct.

"Well done," Rodrigo says. "Caiman are like crocodiles and are one of the most ferocious predators in the Amazon basin. They can grow to over 15 feet in length and weigh more than 800 pounds?"

"I wouldn't want to meet one of those out swimming," you say. "What do they eat?"

Rodrigo laughs. "Anything they can catch! Fish, birds, turtles, small mammals, even people!"

"But," Maria says. "They are also hunted for their skin and meat. So they don't have it all their own way."

"Your clue wasn't much help," you tell Rodrigo. "Anacondas are long and reptiles too."

Rodrigo looks a bit sheepish. "Sorry." Then he turns over another picture. "Here a tough one. What's this?"

Capybara? **P64**
Or
Beaver? **P55**

Capybara is correct.

"Correct," Rodrigo says. "The capybara is the world's largest rodent and a close relative to the guinea pig. They can weigh up to 200 pounds."

"That's a pretty big guinea pig," you say. "Do people eat them?"

"Yup. So do caiman. They're quite social animals and can be found in groups of 100 or more at times."

Then Rodrigo gives Maria a look and raises his eyebrows suspiciously.

She nods.

You wonder what it going on.

"Okay," Rodrigo says. "It's time for your last question. If you get this right you will finish the maze."

"Then you can become a sorcerer's apprentice like us." Maria says. "Won't that be fun!"

"It sure would be nice to learn some of the sorcerer's tricks," you reply. You can just imagine what the kids at school would say when you turn them green, or make spiders appear on their desks.

Rodrigo clears his throat. "Okay here we go. One of these animals isn't found in the Amazon River basin. Can you guess which one?"

Maria holds up her hand. "Be careful. You don't want to end up back at the start now that you're so close."

Rodrigo pulls a bright yellow piece of paper out of his pocket. On it is a list of three animals. He lays it on the table in front of you.

It is time to make a decision. Which of these animals doesn't live in the Amazon River basin?

"Be careful," Maria says. "This could be a trick question."

"Or not," Rodrigo says with a grin on his face.

You read the list. They all seem familiar.

Is it:

Pink Dolphin **P85**

Tarantula **P55**

Or

Leopard **P102**

You have chosen to go to sleep.

You lie down, close your eyes and hope for the best. You're pretty sure the sorcerer won't let anything happen to you. After all, why would he provide you with guides if he didn't care about your safety?

Rodrigo and Maria said they'd be back first thing in the morning. Why would they say that if the sorcerer planned to have you eaten during the night? They don't seem the type to tell fibs.

You dream of gigantic spiders and snakes. A couple of times during the night, you get up and throw extra logs on the campfire to keep the wild animals away.

It feels like you've only just dropped off to sleep, when someone starts shaking your arm.

"Wake up sleepyhead!" Maria says. "My brother's cooking breakfast."

You yawn and swing your legs onto the ground. The

smell of eggs makes your stomach rumble.

Rodrigo has dished up three plates, so you sit at the table and prepare to eat.

"Wait," he says. "Before you get breakfast—"

"Let me guess," you interrupt. "I have to answer a question?"

Rodrigo smiles. "You're getting the hang of this maze stuff. At least the first question in the morning is usually an easy one."

"Well I hope so. I'm starving."

Maria comes and sits beside you. "You can do it. Just think logically."

"Okay here we go," says Rodrigo. "If there are three giant otters, and each otter eats three fish per day. How many fish will the three otters eat in a week?"

It is time to make a decision. Is the correct answer:

61 fish? **P69**

Or

63 fish? **P72**

You have chosen tea.

"Oops," says Rodrigo. "Tea is incorrect. Brazil has over 10,000 square miles of coffee plantations. It's China that grows the most tea, followed by India and Kenya."

"Oh well," you say. "What happens now?"

Rodrigo points to a hammock hanging between two trees.

Maria rests her hand lightly on your shoulder. "Looks like you're sleeping in the hammock tonight.

"But what about wild animals?" you ask. "Won't it be dangerous?"

Maria points to the fire and a stack of wood. She walks over and drops a log onto the burning embers. "Not if you keep the fire going."

You're about to ask more questions when Rodrigo and Maria begin to fade. Then they disappear altogether.

"Hey you two! Don't go yet. I still have questions!"

You wait for one of them to reply, but they've gone. So what now? Do you stay up and sit around the campfire all night, or do you try to get some sleep?

It is time to make a decision. Do you:

Go to sleep? **P66**

Or

Sit around the campfire? **P71**

You have chosen 61 Fish.

"Oh no!" Maria says. "If there are three giant otters, and they eat three fish per day each, that's nine fish per day. Nine fish for seven days equals 63 fish."

"Oops," you say. "I never was that good at math."

"Or you could have worked it out by taking one otter that eats 3 fish per day for seven days. That's 21 fish and 3 times 21 is 63." Rodrigo smiles. "Would you like another question so you can move on?"

"Yes please."

Rodrigo pulls another question from the seemingly endless supply in his pocket. "Okay but don't mess this one up or you'll have to go back to the start of the maze."

"What? Right back to the very beginning?"

"Yep," Rodrigo says, giving you a serious look. "Here we go. If you have 29 fish and add 34 fish. How many fish do you have?"

70

Maria taps you on the shoulder. "Remember you can use a calculator if you need to."

"Where would I find a calculator in the jungle?" you ask.

"Use your fingers and toes then," she says. "Just don't get this one wrong."

Rodrigo smiles. "Adding 9 and 4, the last digit of each number, together might give you a hint about which one is right."

It is time to make a decision.

Is 29 fish plus 34 fish:

63 fish? **P72**

Or

61 fish? **P85**

You have chosen to sit around the campfire.

You are alone in the jungle. The fire is a comfort, but it's also too warm to sit very close to the crackling flames. In the light of the fire, you make yourself another sandwich and think.

There are so many sounds. Mainly frogs, from what you can tell. You wonder if any of the frogs you hear croaking are poison dart frogs. You certainly wouldn't want to touch one of those. They secrete enough deadly poison through their skin to stop a person from breathing.

Occasionally you hear something larger moving through the undergrowth. Could it be an anaconda or jaguar? You're near the river too. Do caiman come out of the river to hunt at night?

Maybe the best thing to do would be to go to bed, get some sleep and be ready for morning.

But what if there are dangerous insects like the Brazilian wandering spider about? They're one of the most venomous spiders on earth. And you've read they're nocturnal! Maybe it would be safer to climb up a tree so you are off the ground. You've seen people do that in the movies. But can't spiders climb trees too?

It is time to make a decision. Do you:

Go to sleep? **P66**

Or

Climb up a tree? **P76**

You have chosen 63 fish.

"Well done," Maria says. 63 fish is correct. Let's eat!"

You tuck in to your breakfast. The toast is crispy and the eggs are done just how you like them. "You're not a bad cook, Rodrigo. Is there any more toast?"

Rodrigo hands you another slice, and then passes you a jar of lime marmalade. "Try this, it's great."

Maria looks over at you. "Brazil produces over 700,000 tons of lime each year."

You spread a thick layer of the sticky, green jelly onto your toast and take a bite. "Didn't the old sailors eat citrus fruit to stop scurvy?"

Rodrigo nods. "Lemons and limes use to be carried on sailing ships. Limes originated in Asia, but now they're grown all around the world."

"This tastes better than grape," you say, after another bite. "But then I'm so hungry almost anything would taste good."

Maria gives you a funny look. "Anything?"

Oh no. Why is she looking at you like that? Has she got some new test in mind?

As you are about to take another bite, there is a puff of smoke and you find yourself holding a sandwich.

"Wow where did that come from?"

"The sorcerer!" Rodrigo and Maria say in unison.

"What's it made of?" you ask.

"Queijo," says Rodrigo.

"But what does that mean in English?"

Then you realize you've been trapped. They are going to ask you a question.

Both Rodrigo and Maria are giggling.

"So what do you think a queijo sandwich is made of?" asks Maria. "If you get the answer right you get to come with us further through the maze."

"And if I get it wrong?"

Maria grins. "You get a big surprise!"

It is time to make a decision. What is queijo?

Is it:

Cheese? **P78**

Chicken? **P46**

Or

Take a chance and go to **P93**

You have chosen 32.

"Well done," says Rodrigo, appearing out of nowhere.

Your eyes go wide. "What are you doing here?"

"It's nearly morning," he says.

"I'm pleased to hear that. It's creepy out here in the dark."

"While I was away I learned a new trick," he says. "It's fun being a sorcerer's apprentice." Rodrigo snaps his fingers and Maria appears.

You step back in surprise. "Wow that's a good trick! Can you teach me?"

"Maybe, but you'll have to become a sorcerer's apprentice first."

"I've been learning tricks too," says Maria. She walks over to the camp kitchen and snaps her fingers. In a puff of green smoke, the table is set and a dozen eggs and bread for toast appears. Maria grins at you. "Seeing I've done the shopping, you two get to make the breakfast."

You snap your finger a couple of times in the hope that some of Maria's magic has worn off on you. But the eggs sit in their carton, uncooked.

Rodrigo looks amused at your feeble attempt. "Poached or fried?"

"Is this a trick question?" you ask. "I don't want to end up back at the beginning of the maze."

Rodrigo shakes his head. "Don't worry, it's not a trick."

You're relieved to hear it. "Fried please."

In a flash, three plates are loaded with golden-brown toast and steaming eggs.

"Hey, why are my eggs flecked with green?" you ask.

Rodrigo smiles. "I like green eggs, don't you?"

You take a small bite. "Yum, parsley."

"It's my own special recipe," Rodrigo says.

You're hungry, so you shovel a forkful of food into your mouth.

"Wait till you try my chocolate popcorn."

You nearly choke on your food. "Chocolate popcorn? Are you serious?"

"Not really. I was just trying to lead into the next question. If you get it right you get to move on to the next part of the maze."

You eat fast, worried that you'll be sent off somewhere before you finish. Around these two, you never know when you'll get your next meal. When the last of your eggs are gone, you turn to Rodrigo and smile. "What happens if I get the question wrong?"

"You might find yourself up a tree," he says with a grin. "Now listen carefully. Cocoa beans are the dried and partially fermented seeds of the cacao tree. That's what chocolate is made from. But where did the cacao tree originate?"

South America? **P86**

Or

West Africa? **P89**

76

You have decided to climb up a tree.

You decide to climb a big tree next to the camp. You grab a piece of rope and a bottle of water and start up. Once you work your way up to the first major branch, the branches are evenly spaced and the climbing gets easier.

Some of the branches are covered in moss, lichens and other tiny plants. There's a whole jungle growing up here. Sometimes there are so many vines and plants it makes getting a grip difficult.

Your head snaps upward when you hear movement in the branches above you. What could it be?

You nearly fall out of the tree when a pair of large yellow eyes stare back at you. Despite the warm sticky air all around you, a shiver runs down your back. Maybe if you don't move whatever it is won't attack.

You freeze, and stare back. The eyes seem oddly familiar somehow.

Then you hear purring. Do jaguars purr? Surely not.

"Meowww!" comes the call from up the tree. The eyes move closer.

You are about to climb back down when there is a rustle of leaves and the cat jump onto the branch beside you and starts rubbing itself against your leg.

"Meowww!"

"What are you doing in the jungle kitty?" you say, scratching the purring cat under its chin. "Are you the sorcerer's cat?"

"Meowww!"

As the cat moves against your hand, greedy for more petting, you notice a collar around its neck. Attached to the collar is a piece of paper.

"I bet I know what this is puss," you say as you remove the paper and turn on your flashlight. "This will be another one of those confounded question."

"Me—owww!"

The writing is small, but you can just make out the words.

It says:

WHAT ARE YOU DOING UP THE TREE? GO TO BED OR I'LL SEND YOU BACK TO THE BEGINNING OF THE MAZE.

The note is signed, The Sorcerer.

What do you do?

Climb down and go to sleep? **P66**

Or

Take a chance and turn to **P85**

You have chosen cheese.

"Well done," Maria says. "Eat your cheese sandwich and then let's go. We've still got quite a lot of ground to cover before we reach the end of the maze."

You stuff the sandwich in your mouth. It could be ages before you get to eat again if you get trapped in the maze somewhere. Better safe than sorry.

Rodrigo and Maria get ready to move on. They are stuffing equipment into packs.

"Aren't we taking the boat?" you ask.

Rodrigo shakes his head. "No the next section is a canopy walk up in the treetops."

You look up at the towering trees all around you. A rope ladder hangs down from one of them. "Are we going to climb up that?" you say pointing towards the ladder.

"Good guess," says Rodrigo. "The sorcerer has made a special walkway so we can discover the variety of wildlife that lives high above the forest floor."

Maria looks up from her packing. "You're not afraid of heights are you?"

You swallow. "It depends."

Maria snaps her fingers and you float up into the air about three feet. "I've been learning a few tricks. If you fall, just yell out my name and I'll snap my fingers. That will stop you from falling."

You feel a little better after seeing Maria's powerful magic. Being a sorcerer's apprentice certainly has its advantages.

After filling water bottles and putting pieces of fruit in your daypacks, the three of you head off towards the rope ladder.

As you near the tree, you look up and spot a narrow bridge running from the tree's upper branches to another platform, on a giant tree about 100 yards away.

"Is that where we're going? It sure is a long way up." you say.

"Don't worry," Rodrigo says. "As long as you follow us and do what we say, you'll be fine."

Like acrobats, Rodrigo and Maria scamper up the rope ladder. Higher and higher they climb.

A parrot flits down from an upper branch and lands on a shrub nearby. "Better get a move on!" it squawks.

You tighten the straps on your pack and start up the ladder. The rope sways a bit as you climb, but before long you are standing next to Maria and Rodrigo high up in the crook of the tree. The swing bridge swoops out over the canopy of the smaller trees below.

"Follow me," Rodrigo says as he steps out onto the bridge.

Maria follows her brother, and then you bring up the rear. The bridge is wobbly, but you soon get used to the movement and time your step to counter the swing.

When you look down, you get a bird's eye view of the jungle. "Wow, this sure gives a different perspective of the rainforest," you say.

80

Birds fly below you over a carpet of green tree tops. In the distance, the Amazon River winds its way into a vast expanse of jungle that stretches as far as the eye can see. On one of the trees below, a family of monkeys sit eating plantains.

When you reach the far platform, Rodrigo and Maria are waiting for you with silly grins on their faces.

"What are you grinning at?" you ask.

Rodrigo reaches for his pocket

"Really? I have to answer questions way up here?"

Rodrigo shrugs. "No. You don't have to. You can do the canopy walk by yourself if you like."

Without waiting for an answer, he reaches for a vine. "Good luck." Then he swings off into the jungle.

Maria grabs a vine. "Oh, and watch out for snakes, they love it up here in the trees." Then she swings off after her brother.

"Snakes? Stop! Wait for me!" you cry out, looking for another vine to swing on. But there are none. You look around the platform. All you see is another bridge leading to a tree further along.

What do you do? Do you:

Go back the way you came? **P81**

Or

Carry on across the next swing bridge? **P82**

You have chosen to go back the way you came.

You start back the way you came. If you go back to the rope ladder, you can climb down and walk the short distance to camp. Once there, you can wait for Rodrigo and Maria to turn up. Surely they won't abandon you in the jungle. After all, isn't it their job to make sure you get through the maze?

But as you step out on the swing bridge to retrace your steps, the bridge is at a funny angle. You peer towards the other end and see why. A large snake has wrapped itself around the handrail and is twisting the bridge to one side. The weird angle doesn't seem to be worrying the snake. It has looped itself around the handrail and is slithering along towards you.

There is a sturdy looking branch just below you. Maybe you should climb down onto that to escape the snake. You might just reach it if you climb over the handrail and hang down. Or should you go across the second bridge and see where it leads?

Whatever you do, it needs to be fast, because the snake has seen you and is slithering your way.

It is time for a quick decision. Do you:

Go across the next bridge? **P82**

Or

Climb down onto the tree branch? **P83**

You have decided to cross the next bridge.

This second bridge is a bit wobblier than the first, but at least you're heading away from that big hungry-looking snake. A parrot lands on the rope railing.

"Hello birdie," you say.

The parrot twists its head sideways and eyeballs you. "Hello birdie!"

"So what now?" you ask the bird.

"How should I know? I'm a parrot!"

"But you just answered me! You're not a normal parrot."

"Snake! Snake! Better get a move on!" the parrot squawks.

You look over your shoulder. The snake is crossing the second bridge after you.

You look around for somewhere to go, but there isn't another bridge to cross. Pinned on the trunk is a sign. It says:

PICK A VINE OR YOU'LL BE LUNCH
ONE KNOT OR TWO? WHAT'S YOUR HUNCH?

Wrapped around the tree trunk are two vines. One has a single knot tied in its end, the other has two knots. You hear a hiss. The snake is close. Which vine do you pick?

(Hint: how many stars are on the Chilean flag?)

Swing on the vine with one knot **P94**

Or

Swing on the vine with two knots. **P93**

You have decided to climb down onto the tree branch.

You climb over the rope railing and get ready to drop down onto the branch below. But out here on the edge of the bridge, everything seems much higher. The bridge sways slightly in the breeze. You feel light-headed and your knees tremble. "Help!"

"Hold my hand!"

It's Maria. She's standing beside you.

"On three, jump with me. Don't worry, I won't let you fall." Maria lets go of the bridge and snaps her fingers.

You
are
F
A
L
L
I
N
G

There is a flash of light, a puff of smoke, and then nothing. The next thing you know, you are sitting on the ground and your dizziness is starting to fade.

"That was a close call," Maria says. "And all because you made a silly choice. I have to give you a really hard question now as punishment. If you get it wrong you'll go back to the very beginning of the maze."

"And if I get it right?"

Maria has a serious expression on her face. "You'll see."

She reaches into a pocket and pulls out a piece of paper. The paper is red and there is a big question mark at the top. "Okay here we go. Think carefully now."

"The Pantanal is a huge wetland in the Amazon basin that is sanctuary to migrating bird species, a breeding ground for hundreds of fish species and home to hundreds of mammals and reptiles. Which of these five choices is the biggest threats to the Pantanal?"

Is it:

Cattle ranching? **P88**

Poaching? **P93**

Commercial Fishing? **P88**

Mining? **P85**

All of the above **P94**

Welcome back to Camp 1

"Welcome back to Camp 1. You got that last question wrong didn't you?" Maria smiles and walks towards an ice chest sitting under the table. "Like another cold soda? You must be thirsty with all this zipping around."

Rodrigo laughs. "The sorcerer is a tough taskmaster isn't he?"

Maria and Rodrigo grab a soda each and the three of you sit down at the picnic table.

"So what now?" you ask.

Rodrigo reaches for his pocket. "You'll have to answer the questions again. At least they'll be easier this time."

"Assuming you've been paying attention," Maria says.

Spreading the paper out on the table in front of him, Rodrigo starts reading. "Okay, here we go again. Brazil is the world's largest producer of what common product. Is it:"

Coffee? **P50**

Or is it

Tea? **P68**

You have chosen South America.

"Good pick," Rodrigo says. "Even though most of the world's cacao is grown in West Africa these days, the cacao plant originated in the Amazon basin of South America."

"So do I win a prize?" you ask.

Maria giggles. "No, but you do get to ride with us in the boat again. We're going hunting for electric eels."

"Really? There are eels that run on electricity here in the Amazon?"

Maria laughs. "They don't actually light up, but they sure can give you a jolt. Some generate over 600 volts. Imagine sticking your finger in an electrical socket, only worse."

"Shocking!"

Maria smiles at your pun. "But they're not really eels, even though they look like one," she says. "They're actually a type of knife fish, which is a cousin of the catfish. They use their electricity for hunting and defense."

Rodrigo chuckles. "Did you know there's an electric eel in Tennessee that has its own twitter account? It automatically sends out a message whenever it lets off an electric charge?"

Your forehead creases and you shake your head. "Do I look that gullible?"

"I'm telling you the truth," Rodrigo says. "The Japanese have also used an electric eel to light up a Christmas tree. Google it."

"I will," you say. "I like learning new things about animals."

Rodrigo raises his eyebrows a couple of times. "Hmmm. Do you just?" He glances over at his sister.

Maria smiles and nods to her brother.

They are up to something and you're not sure you like the looks they're giving each other. "Okay you two, what's going on?"

Rodrigo pulls a piece of paper out of his pocket. "It just so happens the sorcerer has prepared an animal riddle for you. I'm looking forward to seeing how you do with this one. It's a bit tricky."

He holds the paper up and reads:

I MIGHT BE BLUE
OR I MIGHT BE RED
SOMETIMES I'M BLACK
WITH A YELLOW HEAD
YOU'D BETTER WATCH OUT
AND HEAR WHAT I'VE SAID
BECAUSE IF YOU TOUCH ME
YOU COULD END UP DEAD

Rodrigo looks over at you. "So what am I?"

A snake? **P91**

A frog? **P94**

Or

A spider? **P93**

Have another go.

You are partially correct, but there are many threats to the Pantanal. Would you like to try that last question again?

Yes **P84**

Or

No. Take me to the correct answer. **P94**

You have chosen West Africa.

Rodrigo looks at you and shakes his head. "That was a good guess because most of the world's cacao is grown in West Africa these days, followed by Indonesia. But, unfortunately for you, it originated in the Amazon basin of South America."

Rodrigo raises his hand.

You can tell he's about to snap his fingers and send you off somewhere. "Wait—"

POOF!

You are high up a tree on a rickety platform built of branches. What are you meant to do now?

Then you see a small sign attached to a branch. It says:

CHOOSE THE RIGHT VINE AND YOU'LL SWING BACK DOWN
BUT IF YOU CHOOSE WRONG, YOU'LL HAVE A FROWN.

When you look around, you see three vines twisted around the trunk of the tree. One has a single knot tied in its end. Another has two knots, and the third has three knots. But which one do you pick? And what happens if you choose wrong, will you fall to the ground and hurt yourself?

You're studying the vines trying to make a decision when you hear a growl from below. It's a jaguar, and it's climbing up the tree towards you!

A parrot lands on a branch beside you. "Jaguar! Jaguar! Better get moving!"

Quick it's time to choose a vine and swing away before

the jaguar get you!

Which of the three vines do you choose?

(Hint: how many stripes are on the Bolivian flag?)

One knot? **P46**

Two knots? **P93**

Or

Three knots? **P94**

Oops, that's not right.

"The correct answer is frog," Rodrigo says. "The poison dart frog, to be exact. There are over 100 different species of poisonous frogs in the Amazon basin. The natives sometimes use frog poison to dip their arrows in."

"Ouch," you say. "I thought they used curare?"

"They do, but frog poison works too." Then he gives you a sad look. "Unfortunately, because you got the wrong answer, I have to send you off into the jungle again."

He clicks his fingers.

In a flash, you are high up a tree, standing on a small platform built out of branches about as big around as your arm. What are you meant to do now?

Then you see a small sign. It says:

CHOOSE A VINE AND SWING BACK DOWN
BUT IF YOU CHOOSE WRONG, YOU'LL HAVE A FROWN.

When you look around you see three vines twisted around the trunk of the tree. One has a single knot tied in its end, another has two knots and the third has three. But which one do you pick? And what happens if you choose wrong?

You are studying the vines when you hear a hiss below you. It is a huge green anaconda! And it's slithering up the tree towards you. Its tongue flicks in and out of its mouth, tasting your scent.

A parrot lands on a branch beside you. "Snake! Snake! Better get moving!"

Quick- it's time to choose a vine and swing off before the anaconda gets you!

Which of the three vines to you choose?

(Hint: how many colors are there on the Columbian flag?)

One knot? **P46**

Two knots? **P93**

Or

Three knots? **P94**

Welcome back to Camp 1

"Welcome back to Camp 1. You got that last question wrong didn't you?" Maria smiles and walks towards an ice chest sitting under the table. "Like another cold soda? You must be thirsty with all this zipping around."

Rodrigo laughs. "That sorcerer is a tough taskmaster isn't he?"

Maria and Rodrigo grab a soda each and the three of you sit down at the picnic table.

"So what now?" you ask.

Rodrigo reaches for his pocket. "You'll have to answer the questions again. At least they'll be easier this time."

"Assuming you've been paying attention," Maria says.

Spreading the paper out on the table in front of him, Rodrigo starts reading. "Okay, here we go again. Brazil is the world's largest producer of what common product. Is it:"

Coffee? **P50**

Or is it

Tea? **P68**

Congratulations you have reached the final stage of the maze.

"Hooray! You got that right," Rodrigo and Maria say in unison.

"Phew!" you say. "So, what now? More questions?"

Maria rests her hand on your shoulder. "Now you just have one more part of the maze to get through and you can become a sorcerer's apprentice, just like us!"

You give Maria and Rodrigo a smile. "Okay let's do it!"

Maria leads you to a table set up in a clearing and brings out a number of photographs. "All you have to do now it identify these animals."

"I'm pretty good at animals," you say. "Ah but these aren't normal photos," Rodrigo says. "They've been specially made by the sorcerer. And you know how tricky he can get."

Maybe you've spoken too soon. "Tricky how?"

Maria giggles. "You'll see."

She lays a picture face up on the table. "What animal is this?"

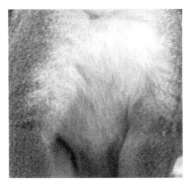

"Hey! Aren't you going to show me all of it! That could be anything!"

Maria shrugs. "I did warn you. The sorcerer never makes it too easy to become an apprentice."

"And," Rodrigo says. "If you get one wrong, you have to go back to the start of this section."

It is time to make a decision. It the picture above a picture of:

A Baboon? **P55**

or

A Spider Monkey? **P56**

List of Choices

More You Say Which Way Adventures

(Available from Amazon.com)

Between The Stars
Pirate Island
Mystic Portal
Dungeon of Doom
Stranded Starship
Dinosaur Canyon
Island of Giants
Creepy House
Lost in Lion Country
Once Upon an Island
In the Magician's House
Secrets of Glass Mountain
Danger on Dolphin Island
Volcano of Fire
Dragons Realm
Deadline Delivery
The Sorcerer's Maze Adventure Quiz (book 1)
The Sorcerer's Maze Time Machine (book 2)

Oops, you've been sent back to the beginning of the maze!

How did you get here? You're back at the jungle clearing.

On the river bank, Maria and Rodrigo stand beside their small boat with the outboard motor attached to its stern and the blue roof to protect its occupants from the hot tropical sun.

Rodrigo waves, "Hello again."

Maria walks towards you. "So, here we are, back at the beginning." she says. "You must have made a really big mistake. Don't worry, my brother and I know the Amazon well, we'll help you through."

"But, as you know, before we go upriver," Rodrigo says, pulling a piece of paper out of his pocket, "the sorcerer wants me to ask you a question. If you get it right, we can leave. At least the answers should be easier to get right this time. Assuming you were paying attention.

"Here goes. How many different species of fish are known to live in the Amazon River?"

It is time to make a choice. Which do you choose?

The Amazon River has over 3000 species of fish. **P4**

Or

The Amazon River has less that 1000 species of fish. **P7**

Congratulations! You made it!

You are suddenly transported up into a massive tree house high in the canopy. It is like nothing you've ever seen. Shelves of books tower to the sky. High above, mighty condors soar amongst the clouds.

In the middle of the room, a boy about your age sits behind a large desk. He is dressed in colorful robes and has a pointy cap on. A jumble of books are open on the desk in front of him.

"So you finally made it," he says.

You nod and then look around. "Are you the sorcerer?"

"Yep!" The boy snaps his fingers. "Abracadabra!" In a puff of pink smoke, a colorful macaw appears on his arm.

The bird tilts its head and stares at you. "Hello birdie!" the macaw squawks. "Took you long enough!"

The sorcerer snaps his fingers again and a comfortable

chair appears. "Take a seat and I'll explain."

The chair is huge and soft, like sitting in a cloud. Then he snaps his fingers again and Rodrigo and Maria appear.

Maria smiles at you and giggles. "This is where the sorcerer makes up all the questions for his mazes. Isn't it a wonderful place?"

You can't help but agree. Never have you seen bookshelves so high. When you look out the window, the jungle stretches for miles in every direction.

The sorcerer gives you a serious glare as he leans forward. "I have so many mazes to make I'm having to do 100 jobs at once. I was hoping you might like to become an apprentice." He snaps his fingers and a cute little spider monkey lands on your lap. "There are lots of benefits you know and to tell you the truth, I could really do with some help."

As you give the monkey a scratch, it wraps long arms around you and gives you a cuddle.

You must admit you're interested. Going through the maze was a lot of fun and becoming one of the sorcerer's apprentices would be exciting. "What would I have to do?"

"You'd help make up the questions for my maze. And every now and then, you get to act as guide for someone new. Like Maria and Rodrigo did for you."

"I can think of lots of cool questions," you say. "Did you know that Pluto is 3,670,050,000 miles from the sun?"

"Hmm... interesting," he says. "You sound like a natural. Maybe you'd like to help me make a maze in space, or one about time travel, or an unusual road trip?" The sorcerer stands up. "You don't have to make your mind up right now."

You give the spider monkey another pat as it picks through your hair looking for fleas.

"I'd better get back to work," the sorcerer says. "I've a million interesting facts to look up."

And with that, the sorcerer disappears in a puff of smoke.

The next thing you know you are back at home, smarter than you were when you left and thinking of all sorts of interesting questions and riddles you'll make up if you decide to become the sorcerer's apprentice.

THE END

For some free bonus previews of more 'You Say Which Way' adventures turn to **P106**

Or you can:

Go to the List of Choice and check for sections of the story you might have missed. **P96**

Please Review This Book

If you enjoyed this book, please remember to review it on Amazon. Reviews help other readers decide if this book is right for them.

Thanks, and may your life be filled with wonderful choices,

The Sorcerer

P.S. for some bonus previews, turn the page.

Free Bonus Previews

Preview: The Sorcerer's Maze - Time Machine

The door is ajar so Matilda gives it a shove and walks into the laboratory. "Hey," she says over her shoulder, "come and look at this."

"Are we allowed?" you ask, stepping cautiously through the doorway. "This area's probably off limits."

"I didn't see a sign," Matilda says, rubbing a finger along the edge of a stainless steel bench as she proceeds further into the brightly lit room. "And if they're going to leave the door open…"

Matilda is a foreign exchange student at your school. She's adventurous and sometimes a little crazy, but she's interesting and the two of you have become good friends.

The rest of your classmates are back in the cafeteria questioning the tour guide about the research facility while they wait for lunch to be served. When Matilda suggested a quick walk, you never guessed she planned to snoop around.

The lab's benches are crammed with electrical equipment. Wires and cables run like spaghetti between servers and fancy hardware. Lights and gauges flicker and glow.

You move a little further into the room. "What do you think all this stuff does?"

Matilda wanders down the narrow space between two benches, looking intently at the equipment as she goes. "I dunno. But they don't skimp on gear, do they?"

A low hum buzzes throughout the room. Most of the components are large and expensive looking. But near the end of one bench, Matilda spots a few smaller pieces of tech.

She prods a brick-sized black box with a row of green numbers glowing across it. "I wonder what this does." She picks it up.

Tiny lights glow above a circular dial. On the top of the box is an exposed circuit board made of copper and green plastic.

"Looks like an old digital clock," you say pointing at the first number in the row. "See here's the hours and minutes, then the day, the month and the year." You pull out your cell phone and check the time. "Yep. It's spot on."

"That makes sense," Matilda says. "But what's the dial for?"

"Beats me. To set an alarm, maybe?

Matilda rubs her finger along a curved piece of copper tubing fitted neatly into one end of the box. "So what's this coil for? Doesn't look like any timer I've ever seen."

When she turns the box over, there is a sticky label on its bottom. It reads:

Hands Off - Property of the Sorcerer

"Who's the sorcerer?" Matilda asks.

You shrug. "A scientist maybe?"

"A sorcerer's a magician, not a scientist." She turns the box back over and starts fiddling with the dial.

You take a step back. "I don't think that's a good—"

A sudden burst of static crackles through the air. The copper coil glows bright red and there's a high-pitched squeal.

FLASH—BANG!

Pink mist fills the air.

"Crikey!" Matilda says. "What the heck caused that?"

Matilda looms ghostlike through the haze.

"We're in for it now," you say, hoping the smoke alarm doesn't go off. "Someone must have heard that."

But as the mist clears, someone hearing you is the last of your worries. "Where—where's the lab gone?"

You're standing on an open plain, brown and burnt by the blistering sun. In the distance, three huge stone structures rise above the shimmering heat haze. Workers swarm over the site like ants on piles of sugar.

Matilda stares, her mouth open, trying to make sense of it all. The black box dangles from her hand. She turns to face you. "Streuth mate! The lab. She—she's completely disappeared!"

"But how? Unless…" You reach down and lift the box so you can check the numbers flashing on its side. "This says it's 11:45."

Matilda nods. "Yeah, that's about right. Just before lunch."

"In the year 2560!"

Matilda's eyes widen. "2560? How can that be?".

"That's 2560 BC," a voice behind you says. "See the little minus sign in front of the numbers?"

The two of you spin around.

"Jeez, mate," Matilda says, glaring at the newcomer. "Where the blazes did you spring from? You nearly scared last night's dinner outta me."

The owner of the voice is a boy about your age, dressed in white cotton. Bands of gold encircle his wrists. His hair is jet black and cut straight across in the front, like his hairdresser put a bowl on his head.

"I'm the sorcerer's apprentice," he says with a smile. "You've been playing with the sorcerer's time machine haven't you?"

"Time machine?" you and Matilda say in unison.

"Welcome to ancient Egypt. The pyramids are coming along nicely don't you think?"

You glance over towards the structures in the distance then back to the boy. "But how did we—"

"— end up here?" the apprentice says. "When you fiddled with the sorcerer's machine, you bent space-time. In fact you bent it so much, you've ended up in the sorcerer's maze. Now you've got to answer questions and riddles to get out."

Matilda's upper lip curls and her eyes squint, contorting her face into a look of total confusion. "What sorta questions?"

The apprentice reaches out his hand. "Don't worry. The questions aren't difficult. But first you'd better give me that box, before you get yourself in trouble."

"Is answering questions the only way to get back?" you ask.

The boy in white nods then gives you a smile. "Here's how the time maze works. If you answer a question correctly you get to move closer to your own time. But if you get it wrong. I spin the dial and we take our chances."

You gulp. "You mean we could end up anywhere?"

"You mean any-when, don't ya?" Matilda says.

The sorcerer's apprentice chuckles. "I suppose you're

right. Anywhere, anytime. It's all the same in the sorcerer's maze."

"But we've got to answer questions to get home?" you repeat. "There's no other way?"

"Sorry, I don't make the rules. I just do what the sorcerer says. At least he's sent me along to help out. That's some consolation, eh?"

"Well… I suppose…"

"Get on with it then," Matilda says in her typical no-nonsense way. "I'm hungry and it's nearly lunchtime."

The boy tucks the black box under his arm, then reaches into a fold of his robe and pulls out a scroll of papyrus. He straightens the scroll and reads. "Okay here goes. The pyramids are about 481 feet high but they weren't used as look out posts or land marks. What was their purpose?"

The apprentice looks at you expectantly. "It's time for your first decision. Which do you choose?"

Did the Egyptians use the pyramids as accommodation for slaves?

Or

Were the pyramids used as tombs?

Preview: The Sorcerer's Maze - Adventure Quiz

Your feet are sinking into a marshmallow floor. You take a few quick steps and find you can stay on top if you keep moving. How did you get here? One moment you were reading and now you are in a long hallway. The place smells of candy and the pink walls are soft when you poke them.

There is a sign hanging from the ceiling that says:

YOU ARE AT THE BEGINNING OF THE SORCERER'S MAZE

But how do you get through to the end of the maze? That is the big question.

Down at the end of the hallway is an old red door. Maybe you should start there?

You take a few bouncy steps, your arms held out to help keep your balance. Getting up would be hard. You don't want to fall.

At last you make it to the red door and try the doorknob. It's locked. You pace in a circle to stop from sinking. When you turn back to the door, you find another sign. On this sign is a question. Below the question are two possible answers. Maybe answering the question correctly will let you open the door.

The questions reads: What is the largest planet in our solar system?

It's time to make your first decision. You may pick right, you may pick wrong, but still the story will go on.

What shall it be? Do you pick:

Jupiter?
Or
Saturn?

[end of previews]